THE
DEAD
DETECTIVE

IN

GHOST CAR 49

THE
DEAD
DETECTIVE

IN

GHOST CAR 49

by Felix Bogarte™

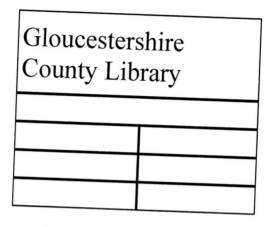

Gloucestershire
County Library

Published 2003 by Books Noir Ltd, Glasgow

Copyright © 2003 Books Noir Ltd

Text written by Joan Love and Mhairi MacDiarmid,
based on a story by Mhairi MacDiarmid

A CIP catalogue for this book is available from the British Library

ISBN 1-904684-05-X

Printed and bound in the EU

www.booksnoir.com
www.deaddetective.com
info@deaddetective.com

CONTENTS

WHO'S WHO IN
DEAD DETECTIVE LAND

WHO IS CHARLIE CHRISTIAN?

12 year-old Charlie Christian is a born detective – and has been given the opportunity to prove himself. The Court Of Ghouls, who exist in a twilight zone between life and death have decreed that the Dead Detective, Hank Kane be sentenced to fight crime in Charlie's very own city of Glasgow! And, as Hank Kane cannot be trusted to solve cases honestly he has been instructed to take on someone he can train as a detective – someone like Charlie Christian.

WHO IS ANNIE?

Ten year-old Annie, or "Ace" as her brother, Charlie, insists on calling her is the world's most reluctant detective. To say that she doesn't share her brother's love of all things detective would be putting it mildly – the whole investigative "scene" bores her senseless.

WHO IS THE GRIM REAPER?

The Grim Reaper, or TG as he likes to be known, really enjoys his work. He loves the perks of his job, annoying Hank, partying and fiddling his expenses.

SO, WHO IS THE DEAD DETECTIVE?

The Dead Detective is Hank Kane, a crooked cop, killed in the line of duty in Los Angeles in the 1950s. Instead of passing straight over to the other side, however, Hank finds himself facing the Court Of Ghouls, who have decided that he'll have to pay for his habit of planting evidence on suspects. They sentence him to fighting crime using only honest methods, until they are convinced that he's learnt his lesson. They instruct The Grim Reaper to keep an eye on Hank. It isn't that they don't totally trust Hank – it's just that they don't trust him at all!

Hank's other problem is his appearance. He's a skeleton! During daylight hours he has no flesh on his bones (well, he *is* dead!) and so has to stay out of sight. At night, however, providing he drinks some of his chemical compound, flesh returns to his bones and he looks almost normal. "Almost" because Hank died fifty years previously and has been catapulted forward in time to 2003.

CHAPTER ONE

KILLING TIME

The Dead Detective, Hank Kane, turned on the TV in his office. A young reporter called Natasha Rose was interviewing, Lorraine Scott, the well-known presenter of a primetime show. They were outside Cowcaddens Studios in Glasgow, the studio that broadcasts many of the Scottish TV shows.

"So tell us, Lorraine," asked Natasha eagerly, "what exactly happened to you here last night?"

"Well," replied Lorraine slowly, in order to get as much publicity from the incident as possible, "I had just picked up my handbag and was leaving the set when it simply *flew* out of my hand! Yes, you heard me, *flew* out of my hand! It was thrown over to the other side of the studio! It was really frightening, I can tell you, as I was on my own. Security arrived when they heard my cry for help and obviously I told them exactly what had happened."

"And did they think you were mad?" asked Natasha, trying to keep a straight face.

Lorraine Scott looked at her in disgust.

"Certainly not!"

"Well it can't be every day that security come across spooky stuff like that," persisted Natasha.

"Actually," said Lorraine, lowering her voice, "things like that are happening almost every day around here. Everyone who works here at night has some strange tale to tell."

"So you're saying the place is haunted," said Natasha, trying to put words in the presenter's mouth. But Lorraine was a professional.

"No! I'm just saying that bizarre things happen around here, that's all."

"Caused by ghosts," said Natasha. She was like a dog with a bone.

"I never said…" Lorraine was beginning to wish she'd just kept her mouth shut and never mentioned her flying handbag. But ratings were ratings and a bit of spare publicity never went amiss.

"Well viewers, there you have it," Natasha continued, "Lorraine Scott admits that she believes in ghosts and is convinced that the studios here are haunted –"

Lorraine was trying desperately to get the cameraman to focus on her but the cheeky swine was pretending not to notice her. Listening to Natasha's wrap up had made her blood boil. "Lorraine Scott is convinced that the studios are haunted..." What a nerve! She had said nothing of the kind! That Natasha person should be kicked right back to whatever local rag she'd scribbled stories for before she hit the big time.

In the meantime, Natasha could barely keep the grin from her face. She had the story she wanted. She could see the headline already. "National Studio – A Ghost of its Former Self!" She kept moving in order to keep the wildly protesting Lorraine Scott out of the shot and delivered her last line.

" – and with that, it's back to you at the studio, Sally."

Back in the studio, Sally Green was sitting at her desk. "And that's all we have time for today. And now the weather..."

At the very mention of the weather, Hank turned off the TV. You didn't need to be a weather forecaster to know what the weather in Glasgow was going to be like, thought Hank. Unless of course you wanted to know exactly what *kind* of rain you were going to get;

torrential rain, light rain, drizzly rain, moderate to heavy rain, rain with sunny periods (the kind that teased you into taking your coat off just so a downpour could soak you to the skin seconds later). Hank had become an expert on rain since coming to Glasgow.

"How do you know when it's summer in Glasgow, Hank?" TG, Hank's companion, often asked him.

"Dunno," Hank would reply wearily, setting up the overly familiar punchline for TG.

"Because the snow turns to rain!" TG still found that one funny, even though he said it every day.

The Dead Detective was killing time. TG had said he'd have a new case for him to investigate. TG, officially known as 'The Grim Reaper', provided most of Hank Kane's cases. After all, The Grim Reaper collected the souls of people when they died. So he had access to as many murder cases as he liked.

The cases he normally asked Hank to investigate usually involved missing money or missing jewellery. While TG could simply find the missing valuables himself, he liked to keep his hands clean, at least, as clean as The Grim

Reaper's hands could be. So, Hank unknowingly often did TG's dirty work.

Just then, TG breezed into Hank's office. He flopped down into Hank's sofa, his long, black cloak billowing around him like a sail. He dropped his scythe on the floor beside him. Hank was about to tell him to put it away in the cupboard as he was always tripping over it, but decided he couldn't be bothered.

"Did you see the news, Hank?" asked TG.

"Sure did."

"I don't mind telling you, Hank, I don't like it when our ghostly comrades start messing with the living. Can't they see what a great thing we have going here?"

"You mean what a great thing *you* have going here."

TG looked hurt. Didn't Hank realise how happy all the ghosts in Glasgow were since The Grim Reaper had started to look after their welfare? Why, he'd even nicknamed the city 'Ghostgow'. Ghosts were coming to the place in their droves. The trains were full of them.

"I mean," TG continued, "they've now got *The Cesspit* nightclub, an establishment that *I* set up for them. Imagine! A nightclub for ghosts to meet up, exchange phone numbers, have a laugh. And if that wasn't enough, I started Dead Guy TV, the TV channel exclusive to the ghost community! And let me tell you, we at The Grim Group Ltd, are still expanding. Last week we launched *The Daily Ghost*, incorporating *Ghoul*, I might add, The Magazine for Fashion Conscious Corpses. In this month's issue we're doing a special, 'Would You Be Seen Dead In This?' feature. Radio Deadbeat is going really well, so what more could they want? But, hey, they still need to go around haunting the living. I mean, its just so passé, so last year."

Hank listened to TG's rant. He knew why TG was unhappy. All TG's ideas for ghosts had made Glasgow the ghost capital of Europe. As always when a lot of folk arrive, there's a few mischievous ones who don't play by the rules. Hank also knew that the Court Of Ghouls frowned on haunting or any other activities that might make the living aware of the ghosts in their midst.

"Don't these guys realise," continued TG, "that they'll bring the Court Of Ghouls down on us like a ton of bricks! And then they'll be sorry. No more nightclubs, TV channels, nothing. Just back to what it was like before. Dead. 'Pure Dead Nothing', to use a Glasgow expression."

Hank stood up to stretch his legs. He stepped over TG's scythe and wandered over to the window. He looked out at all the people; running to catch trains, shopping, meeting one another. Add sunshine and smiles and it could be downtown LA, thought Hank. Not that Hank had a clue what LA looked like nowadays. After all, he'd been dead for fifty years. Maybe the sound of Glasgow's traffic was like the faint meow of a pussycat compared to the monstrous roar of LA's snarled-up traffic-jams. TG was still complaining, giving it loads.

"Ghosts of today, no manners, no respect…I'm telling you, Hank, this neighbourhood is going down the pan!"

"What did you expect, TG, when you opened all these attractions? I thought you wanted this to be the capital of Europe for ghosts? Sure, didn't you give its new nickname, 'Ghostgow'?"

"I did. I did. But I thought maybe I could screen the ghosts that turned up. I *am* 'The Grim flipping Reaper' after all. I collect the souls of everyone who dies – well *almost* everyone who dies - obviously I have to franchise out some of the work. But the thing is, a few of my employees are getting sloppy. Professionalism, Hank, it's getting rarer. You just can't get the staff these days."

Hank walked back over to his desk to use the phone.

"Who're you calling, Hank?" asked TG, grinning, "Ghostbusters?"

"Very funny," said Hank, clearly not in the mood for TG's attempts at humour, "I'm giving Charlie and Annie a call. I presume you're going to tell me about a case you want solved."

"Tell them to come tomorrow. I'll explain it all then but right now I need to meet my publisher. They're publishing my autobiography!" said TG, getting up off the sofa and heading for the door. "I take it you'll be at *The Cesspit* tonight?"

Hank nodded as he picked up TG's scythe and handed it to him as he left. Dumb reaper was always forgetting it. He got Charlie on his mobile and they agreed to meet the following evening. Charlie had complained about having to bring his kid sister but Hank had insisted.

"You guys work best as a team," he'd said.

The team Hank referred to was the 'Charlie and Annie' detective team. Charlie was twelve years old and Annie was ten. Hank was training them in the art of detecting, as he'd been instructed to do by the Court Of Ghouls.

Bad guys, and even good guys who just happened to have made mistakes, often found themselves in front of the Court Of Ghouls when they died. The Court decided if they could pass over to the other side. In Hank's case, this meant passing into Detective Heaven, where even the hardest cases are solved easily. However, as Hank had been caught cheating on a case back in 1950s LA, the Court had sentenced him to going back to earth to solve crime honestly.

Why Glasgow? Well, the Court had simply spun a globe and one of the judges had closed his eyes and picked a place at random. His finger just happened to land on Glasgow. It could have been anywhere. The Grim Reaper had been asked to 'keep an eye' on Hank. Hank had come to realise, that it was *he* who needed to keep an eye on The Grim Reaper. And who, in their right mind, would volunteer for that task?

CHAPTER TWO

CHARIOTS ON JAMACIA STREET

HANK lay awake in bed, watching the walls of his bedroom change colour. Every time the traffic lights outside changed from red, to amber, to green and all over again, the walls changed colour with them.

Hank didn't like curtains. He wanted to feel part of the night. He didn't worry about people seeing in. Okay, so they'd have to be sitting in the top of a double-decker bus to see in, but he wouldn't have worried even if his bedroom was on the ground floor. As TG had often explained, the only people who could see Hank's office at all were either people who Hank had invited, or those who TG had sent.

Hank hadn't gone to *The Cesspit* tonight after all. The place was far too busy nowadays. The guys selling sarsaparilla were happy, the dudes selling tacky, 'I had a Dead Good Time At The Cesspit' T-shirts were happy – everyone was happy except those who fancied a quiet time.

TG was right, thought Hank. The city was

getting noisier. Not that the living made more noise than usual. No, this noise was a result of Glasgow attracting ghosts from all over the world, in search of a good time. They came from all periods of history, too. Some raced chariots down Jamaica St, some raced fighter jets in the skies. There was a tour group of Vikings due over next week and the stag nights and hen parties were really lowering the tone of the place. The ghost cops turned a blind eye to a lot of what went on but it was all getting out of hand.

Hank flicked on the radio at his bedside. He was just in time to hear the midnight news.

"Radio Deadbeat news at midnight. Read by Jasper Leitch. A clerk at the Court of Ghouls, Mr A. Clarke, was arrested today on suspicion of First Degree Haunting. The target of his haunting, a psychic, Mr Rory Gunn had turned the tables on him by screaming 'BOO!' until the ghost police arrived. This brings the number of ghosts arrested for haunting this month to twenty but it's the first time that an official at the Court has been implicated..."

Hank had the feeling that things were

beginning to spiral out of control where the ghost population in Glasgow was concerned. But why all the hauntings? Why now? Was it really just down to an increase in the number of ghost tourists? Maybe. Something would have to be done. In the meantime, the news continued:

"Sports news now, and in the Severed Head Basketball Championships today, the Glasgow Gangsters tied with the Barcelona Basket-Cases…"

Hank had never been into sports. Even his signed picture of Joe Di Maggio was a gift from someone who didn't really know him. He turned down the radio and almost dozed off. Just before he fell asleep, however, he was woken up by the sound of screeching tyres and machine guns firing, all to the sound of jazz music blaring out from a car radio!

"What the …" Hank jumped out of bed and ran over to the window. He looked out and saw a 1950s car, doing wheel spins on the pedestrianised area of Gordon Street outside Central Station. The passengers in the car were leaning out through the windows and firing bullets at all and sundry!

The car was obviously a ghost car of some description but the people on the street were regular living people, not ghosts. They could obviously see the ghost car as they were screaming, running for their lives and diving out of the way of the bullets!

This was definitely not normal. What usually happened when ghosts had a row was that they'd fight, but it would all be unseen by "Alive Guys" as ghosts sometimes called humans. This meant that humans didn't get hurt and most importantly for the ghost community in Glasgow, the 'Alive Guys' wouldn't realise that there was a complete ghost city running parallel to everyday life!

But tonight, Hank had just witnessed what could well be the beginning of the end of TG's dream city for ghosts. The minute humans got hurt by ghosts, the Court would get involved. And the Court would err on the side of caution. They'd close down all of TG's operations and Glasgow would be a deadzone for ghosts once more. Would that be a bad thing, wondered Hank? Well, it'd certainly mean a guy could get a decent bit of kip without being woken up by a bunch of deadbeats practising drive-by shootings!

Hank checked the news each hour before dawn. Amazingly, there was no mention of the incident at all. Sounded suspiciously like a news blackout to Hank.

Hank took the cup of coffee Charlie offered him. He was sitting in his leather chair, listening to TG explain the situation to him and his assistants. He watched them carefully to make sure they were listening.

"So," said TG, "I think I know what's going on."

"There's a surprise!" laughed Charlie.

"This is serious, kid, this really could be the end of civilisation as we know it!" said TG. "I've put a few measures in place to calm this city down. Number one: the ghost police will deport anyone even suspected of haunting. Number two: my technicians have invented a spirit force field that means no new ghosts will be able to find Glasgow. It's off the ghost map until things settle. Decent upstanding Glaswegian ghosts will be accepted of course. But even then, they will be screened. In short, the only way in and out this city will be through me, and my most trusted staff."

"So," asked Charlie, "where do me and Ace come in?"

"Annie," corrected his sister, automatically. Charlie insisted on calling her 'Ace'. TG's line of thought was thrown for a second but he continued.

"Well, while you guys are working for Hank and I, you can see everything ghosts can see. You've seen the Court Of Ghouls, right? There's nothing scarier than that so you've nothing left to fear. What I need you guys to do is look out for ghosts that are haunting humans. Keep Hank up to date with any you find. It's time to clean up this city. Hank, if I remember rightly, that's something you're very good at!"

"Is that it? Is that all you have to say?" asked Hank.

"What do you mean 'is that it'? The city's falling apart, Hank! What more do you want?"

"I just thought, TG, you might have had some specific incident you'd want to go over with us, that's all."

TG thought for a moment. He looked as if he was weighing up the odds, thought Hank, trying to guess what Hank knew and what Hank didn't know.

"What makes you say that Hank? Did somebody say something at *The Cesspit* last night?" asked TG.

"No," replied Hank.

So, TG thought Hank was at *The Cesspit* last night. He wouldn't know that Hank had stayed in and witnessed for himself the gangster car shoot out right under his window. Now it was Hank's turn to gamble. Did TG know that Hank was holding out on him? Why didn't TG just come out and ask Hank what 'specific incident' he was hinting at? Hank thought for a moment then decided to keep that information to himself. TG looked like he expected Hank to say more – and was a little surprised when he didn't.

However, TG was under a lot of pressure at the moment. He had to hope his measures were enough to calm the city down, or risk The Grim

Group Ltd going out of business. He was halfway out the door when Annie shouted after him.

"Hey, TG, you forgot these!" Annie handed him his brief case and his phone. He thanked her, looking a little embarrassed. This wasn't the master of efficiency they'd come to know as TG. This was more like some scatty professor, with too much on his mind.

CHAPTER THREE
THE ETHERJUICE RACKET

CHARLIE, Annie and Hank sat in a corner of *The Coffee Shop* in Glasgow's Central Station. They sat in the area reserved for ghosts. Not that humans had a clue that the corner was reserved for ghosts. All they knew was that it stank. Even the waitress refused to bring them their drinks – Charlie had to collect them from the bar. The other customers wondered why on earth anyone would want to sit there! Charlie and Annie asked Hank the same question.

"The thing is guys, as TG explained to me before you arrived, ghosts are now restricted to certain areas of pubs, restaurants, coffee houses etc. There has just been too many hauntings, just one too many irresponsible ghosts. We're here so that I can talk to a particular ghost."

"What about?" asked Annie.

"We're on a case, guys."

"Are we, Hank?" asked Charlie, "I don't remember TG talking about an actual *case*. He just told us to keep our eyes open, didn't he?"

"Yep, that's right. That's all he said. That's *why*

we're on a case. It's what TG *didn't* say that tells me that." Hank told Charlie and Annie about the car and the guns outside his window the night before.

"But Hank," said Annie, "there's nothing unusual about that kind of behaviour from ghosts these days."

"But why didn't TG want to talk about that specific incident if there was nothing unusual about it? That's the question. See, that car is connected to TG and both are connected to something rotten."

"TG is always up to some scam," said Charlie, "what's so strange about this one?"

"TG's scams are money making ventures. Now I'm not going to stop some guy making a living. But something tells me The Grim Reaper has gone too far this time. Something tells me he's lost control of this city. And we gotta find out what's happened. And, by the way, we can't tell TG we're on this case, OK?"

Charlie and Annie nodded, even if they were a little worried. Hank didn't feel comfortable being this frank with his assistants but they were 'Alive Guys', so they were not yet in the pocket of TG, who had every dead person in his debt. So he knew he could trust Annie and Charlie. Well, he knew he *had* to trust them because he sure as heck couldn't trust anyone else.

Just then, the ghost of Alan Hendy arrived, apologising for being late. "Flipping security checks are causing ghost-jams all over the city, Hank," he said, pulling up a chair and sitting down.

Hendy had been a mad scientist who'd blown himself up in his lab one night as he tried to develop a potion that he could give to his local football team. His team had been getting thrashed every week and as he'd supported them from a time when he was sane (a very, long time ago indeed), he felt obliged to help. Unfortunately, his grasp of chemical compounds was as bad as his team's grasp of football and so he went up in smoke. To make matters worse, his team were relegated, making it a very poor season, all things considered.

Hank had met Hendy recently when he'd knocked on the office door. Hank had been surprised because normally only people who've been invited by Hank or TG can find the office (it's hidden from everyone else). But in these crazy times, all the ghostly rules were falling apart.

Hendy had been selling flesh-restoring potions, like the ones Hank had, door-to-door. Hank had busted him, as it was illegal to possess the stuff without a licence from TG. Hendy had protested that he had a licence but it was 'in the post'.

Hank hadn't bought that story for a second and had personally dropped him at the Court Of Ghouls. TG had thanked Hank as he'd taken Hendy up the stairs to the Court. But Hank had been surprised when he hadn't been called to give evidence and even more surprised when he'd heard nothing about the case on Radio Deadbeat or anywhere else. And when he'd seen Hendy in *The Cesspit* one night, he couldn't work out why he wasn't behind bars.

"Well, Dr Hendy," asked Hank, "what's going on in this mad city?"

"I tell you Hank, this city's morals are decaying quicker than your flesh!" he said as he ruffled his spiky, red hair. He looked every bit like the mad scientists you'd see in cartoons.

"Let's get one thing straight, Hendy," said Hank, "I'm not buying any of your darn potions! We'll just stick to the case, okay?"

"You must already have a dealer then," said Hendy, in a sly voice.

"A dealer!" exclaimed Hank, "what do you take me for, Hendy? I get mine – "

" – on prescription from TG," they both said in unison, much to Hank's surprise.

"That's what they all say, Hank," said Hendy. "I tell you, ghosts just love that stuff. There's a racket going on where that potion is concerned. That's all I can tell you."

"What's a 'racket' Hendy?" asked Annie.

"He means people are trading in the potion illegally," said Charlie, delighted to be able to tell Annie something she didn't know.

"That's right, son," said Hendy, unaware that Charlie hated the term 'son' only slightly less than 'kid'.

"How'd that happen, Hendy?" asked Hank. "I thought TG had the manufacture of that stuff very tightly controlled."

"He did, but he loosened the controls a little. That made the ghosts come back to Glasgow, and they brought their friends. *And* they brought their ghost money, too. See, TG thought he was just enticing more ghost tourists to the city but when they demanded the potion, he told them 'no'."

"Yeah, that adds up. TG might be enterprising but I can't see him being that irresponsible. He's not stupid. He'd have known that selling too much of the potion would get out of control. And we know how TG loves control," said Hank.

"Right. But these visiting ghosts were determined. They wanted supplies. And TG wouldn't do it, so that's where I came in. People knew I could help."

"You? How could you help? Did they want to blow themselves up?" laughed Charlie.

Hank looked at him with disdain. Dr Hendy continued as if he hadn't even heard Charlie's remark.

"You think TG invented that potion, Hank? He didn't. I did. The only mistake I made was selling him the compound in return for him fixing it so that my team won football's Scottish Cup. That was back in 1958. The Court of Ghouls told TG to keep the compound a secret. It was a revolutionary medicine. I called it 'Etherjuice' and it changed the lives of hundreds of ghosts. It would have changed a lot more lives if TG hadn't kept it under wraps. So I started to dish out my own brand. Only to desperate cases, though."

"Why not let all ghosts have access to Etherjuice?" asked Charlie.

"It kept the price high. TG could sell it sparingly and still make money. But the reason the Court Of Ghouls wanted it hushed up was ...well imagine, all the ghosts in the world being visible to humans all the time. Because that's what you'd get. There would be panic! Even in a perfect world, there would be ghosts who didn't know what dosage to take. So they'd be walking around without a care in the world while humans fainted at the sight of them as their flesh either fell off 'cause they hadn't taken enough Etherjiuce, or they would burst into flames if they took too much!"

"Wow! That would really scare us humans," commented Charlie.

"It wouldn't do much for us ghosts either!" said Hendy. "Listen Hank," he continued, "the potion *you* have is a variation of my compound. You are the only ghost who can operate in both the human and ghost worlds. But see, even though you busted me, I know you're a trustworthy, responsible guy. So I think, it's okay for guys like you to have that potion. But what about some of those guys down at *The Cesspit*. Imagine if *they* could operate in both worlds! It would be chaos!"

"It's almost chaos now. So what can we do about this, Hendy? Who are the big players in this Etherjiuce racket?"

"No names, Hank. That was our deal, remember? You carry a lot more weight than I do in this town. I'm a just a mad scientist. Meeting you is all the risk I wanna take."

"Wait a minute, Hendy. I bet I could find something to book you on. I need some clues. Or even one clue! You've given me nothing to go on. Tell me, who is running the Etherjuice racket?"

Silence.

"Alright. So you won't give me a name. What if I give *you* a name? If it's right, you just nod your head, OK?"

Hendy agreed. Here goes, thought Hank, as he prepared to say the name he dreaded might be behind this whole thing. He looked Hendy straight in the eye. "Is it TG?" he asked.

Hendy shook his head.

Hank, Charlie and Annie were all very surprised - and very relieved. No one wanted to take on TG. Hank knew he'd have to one day but he always hoped that day would be 'tomorrow' and never 'today'.

"Don't get too cheered up," said Hendy, "when you see who it is, you'll wish it *was* just TG you were dealing with!"

"What do you mean?" demanded Hank.

"One TG is bad enough, right? So try a car full of TGs!"

Charlie gasped. Annie nearly choked on her drink. Hank's heart sank. It looked like 'tomorrow' had finally arrived... today.

CHAPTER FOUR

"THIS IS A RAID!"

BACK in his office, Hank tried TG's mobile number again. Still no answer. He tried Charlie's. Charlie picked up.

"Listen, Charlie," Hank warned, "keep away from this neighbourhood tonight. There might be trouble."

"That's why I should be there, Hank."

"No, that's why you *shouldn't* be here. I need you to operate in the human world. I want you to look out for signs that ghosts are becoming visible to humans. At the first sign we see that things really are about to collapse around us, we go straight to the Court Of Ghouls. Remember, you me and Annie are the only ones who can operate in both worlds. Let's do our best to keep it that way. Where is Annie?"

"She's at the TV studios, where you told her to be."

"Did she get in?"

"Of course. You've taught us all about 'bluffing'. But don't ask me how she did it."

"How do you know she's in place?"

"I just called her. She has your mobile, remember, the one you don't know how to work?"

"Okay, okay, wise guy! Has anything unusual happened yet?"

"Don't think so. What did you say's going to happen, again?"

Hank held the receiver away from his face, screaming silently in frustration. Okay, keep calm. He'd try one more time to explain.

"My hunch is that some ghost will try to hijack the newsroom."

"Oh yeah, I remember… why, again?"

"Concentrate Charlie! Because this particular bunch of ghosts want to bring complete chaos to the world. Bad guys can't take over a well-ordered world. They have to create complete chaos. Then there's no law. And without the law, they can do what they like. Now, if they can somehow broadcast false news to the world, like, say, they tell the world that Russian troops have just invaded Poland, or America fired missiles at France… if they manage to broadcast stuff like that to the human world, there would be chaos, right?"

"But why do that from little, old Glasgow? They could do it from anywhere!"

"No they couldn't. Glasgow's the only city in the world where ghosts are roaming high on Etherjuice. And TG has the ghost boundaries of Glasgow secured. Remember he'd told us that no ghost can get in or out of the city. You've seen the queues. You can bet he doesn't want any of this to get out. He'd be finished."

"So Annie's to watch for ghosts posing as humans, ghosts that have taken Etherjuice to make them look normal."

"Good Charlie. Now you're on the ball. Now I want you to go to Queen Margaret Drive, where the other TV station is, okay? Do the same there as Annie's doing at Cowcaddens, right?"

"Right!"

Hank replaced the receiver and ran quickly, chased by the rain, to the cash points in Buchanan Street. In the old days, before this ghost crisis, only a handful of people had known the code to punch-in to gain access to *The Cesspit*. But now even the likes of Tony Falco knew the code. Everyone seemed to know the code except Hank, or so it seemed to him.

Falco was a dead jewel thief, who Hank had helped enter 'Bandit Heaven'. This was a place where even the dumbest thieves could steal the most valuable jewels all day long, without getting caught. But Tony knew he owed Hank Kane big-time and so he'd been persuaded to come back and repay him.

A few streets ahead, Hank could see Tony waiting for him right where he said he'd be – beside the cash points. As Hank ran towards him he could see Tony shivering and pulling his jacket collar up around his neck to keep out the rain. Hank ran faster, all the time watching as Tony tried to dodge the driving rain that nearly swept him against the wall of the building. When Hank finally reached him, they shook hands and instantly began moaning about the weather.

"Told you to bring an overcoat," said Hank, almost shouting over the din of the rain.

"Overcoat? Didn't exactly do *you* a lot of good – you're soaking, Hank!" shouted Falco, despite being just in front of Hank.

As they were getting ready to punch in the numbers into the cash point, a group of guys dressed like 1950s New York gangsters, pushed past them. They punched in some numbers and ran inside as the wall opened for them. Hank and Tony tried to run in behind them but the last guy turned round and shouted at them. "Where the heck d'you think you're going, losers?" and slammed the wall shut in their faces.

Hank was more bothered about the rain than by the insult but Tony looked shaken as he fumbled about with the cash point's buttons, trying some numbers.

"What's happened to this town, Hank?" he asked, yelling in order to be heard above the downpour that crashed onto the streets.

"What *hasn't* happened, Tony? It would be easier to answer *that* question," said Hank. He noticed that Tony was trying a range of different numbers. "What's wrong, Tony," he asked, "can't you get the numbers right?"

"I got 'em alright. But the code's been changed, Hank!"

Hank groaned and looked up towards the heavens. Big mistake, he thought, as the rain drenched his face.

"Can't we get in, Tony?"

Tony thought for a moment. He knew a way of doing this but breaking and entering wasn't strictly legal, not even in TG's ghost world. He looked at Hank as rain now poured down both their faces. Hank nodded.

"Do it Tony, just do it!" shouted Hank. A bus went past, skilfully managing to hit the exact spot in a puddle that meant Hank and Tony were hit by a gigantic splash. And in that very second, Tony got the door to open. Hank didn't want to know how.

They stood in the spruced-up lobby of *The Cesspit* trying to catch their breath. The howling wind and the pounding rain banged against the wall outside the nightclub. Hank was sure the wall wouldn't be strong enough to keep the elements from bursting through it. The weather sounded like it was angry, as if it had been robbed of some fun.

Puddles of rain formed at their feet as they stood in the lobby. Hank felt like an intruder, even though he'd been a regular customer at *The Cesspit* from the night it first opened its doors. Back then *The Cesspit* had been a real dive, truly revolting. But it had been peaceful. Now, what with the ghost tourists to cater for, the lobby looked like the lobby of a five star hotel. Except it was empty.

"You got the stuff, Tony?"

Tony gave Hank four small bottles.

"Will this be enough, Hank?" asked Tony concerned.

"Don't worry. I know the inventor real well. Now follow me."

As they made their way down the corridor, the noise they heard sounded like one hell of a party. It was coming from the bar. Hank and Tony suspected the new customers might not welcome their uninvited guests. They got to the door of the bar and opened it slightly. Hank had to squint to see through all the smoke.

"Anyone we know, Hank?"

"Don't think so."

"Don't tell me it's full of tourists!"

"Not just tourists, Tony."

"So what have we got in there?"

"Bootleggers, Tony. Etherjuice bootleggers. They look like the members of the Micciano family. Something tells me the good Doctor Hendy let them into his Etherjuice secrets."

"But Hank, I thought you wiped out all the Micciano family at that shoot out in LA?"

"Doesn't do us much good now though; looks like their ghosts must be running this racket. Hold on to your hat, Tony. I've just appointed you Deputy."

"And who appointed you Sheriff?"

"Me."

"When?"

"Two seconds ago. Now c'mon, get ready to bluff! Here take this," said Hank, handing Tony back one of the little bottles.

"What kind of Etherjuice is *this*, Hank?" asked Tony, inspecting the bottle.

"Not the kind you get on prescription from TG, that's for sure. C'mon, let's go!"

And with that Hank burst into the bar of *The Cesspit* with a very confused Tony Falco following him. The band stopped playing and everyone stopped talking to get a good look at the two soaking wet figures who'd just burst in.

"Freeze everybody! This is a raid!"

Everybody laughed and the band started up again as if no one had even heard Hank. Hank took one of the special bottles of Etherjuice out of his pocket. He looked around the room for Massimo Micciano, head of the crime family. He spotted him pointing at him and laughing. Hank aimed his bottle at Massimo Micciano and threw it with all his might. Direct hit! BOOOOMMMMM!!! Massimo blew up into millions of tiny pieces, no use to anyone now, not even as a ghost! Hank was stunned.

"Dr Hendy doesn't lie!" he said out loud.

Tony, standing beside Hank, was most encouraged. He looked at some guys who'd wondered over in his direction.

"You want some? Well do you, punk!"

The guys backed off.

"That's better, fellas!" shouted Hank. "Well, now that I've got your attention, let me just repeat what I said. I said THIS IS A RAID!! Everybody got that? Good!"

Hank pulled another two bottles from his pocket. He held them up for the crowd to see. "Let me tell you low-lifes something. These bottles are NOT, I repeat, NOT, Ghost Government Issue, okay? These little babies are Dr Hendy's own brand!"

A muffled 'ooh' went through the crowd and

everyone took a step back. A couple of guys who had put their right hands inside their jackets now took them out, sensibly leaving their guns where they were. Hank felt safer.

"Yeah," he said, "Dr Hendy doesn't mess about. He's got me some real dangerous stuff." Hank walked around, teasing the crowd. "Such a dedicated scientist. He went through twenty different experiments to get me this stuff. What a scientist, I tell you! I'm not saying he looks as pretty *tonight* as he did this morning – but hey, that's science. Now all you law abiding tourists, you ain't got anything to worry about. I know city security won't let you leave just yet. But the quicker I solve this case, the case of the Etherjuice bootleggers that is, the quicker we can *all* go home, comprendez? Now, all you no-good bootleggers, you have Hank Kane to worry about. Tony, check behind the bar. Something tells me there's more than sarsaparilla coming out of those beer taps."

As Tony went behind the bar, he heard some of the bad guys in the crowd whispering. "We know you, Falco, we've got friends in Bandit Heaven. We'll sort you out." Undisturbed, Tony put his finger to one of the taps and then to his mouth and licked it. "*Very* watered down Etherjuice, Hank. Looks like this place has been ripping everyone off!"

The crowd erupted in anger and tried to rush the bar to get at the remaining Micciano gang members who were leaning against it.

"Looks like we ain't gonna be short of witnesses, fellas! Thanks, Tony."

Marco Micciano stepped forward. "There's nothing wrong with the Etherjuice here, I can guarantee that we only sell the best of it! You have my word!"

"Thanks, Marco," shouted Tony, "Can't beat a taped confession, huh?" and he held up a small cassette, the kind you find in a dictaphone.

The crowd burst into laughter, and the other Micciano brothers glared at their thick brother, who had surely got them well and truly caught in the act. It seemed that in the heat of the moment, only Hank and Tony were aware of the obvious. To tape something onto a dictaphone cassette, you also need a dictaphone. Hank had to admit, Tony Falco was a natural when it came to bluffing.

The ghost police arrived and marched the Micciano brothers off.

"This establishment is now closed until further notice, by order of the Court Of Ghouls," announced the Sergeant.

A team of guys from Forensics arrived and combed the place looking for clues. One of them rushed up to the Sergeant with something in his hand.

"Well?" asked Sergeant Galloway looking at the guy's hand, "You're gonna have to tell me what it is, son!"

"Etherjuice burns Sarge. Looks like Grade Z Etherjuice, too. The bottle this was in would have exploded like a nuclear hand grenade!"

"What are you saying, son?"

"This isn't the government issue Etherjuice that the Miccianos were bootlegging, Sarge. If you drank this, you'd disintegrate."

"Oh, you mean it's like poteen?"

"Like what, Sarge?"

"Nothing. Go on."

"This stuff is a new brew, Sarge. If more of this gets out – boy, we really are in trouble."

Sergeant Galloway stroked his chin. He'd been

in the SES (Special Etherjuice Squad) for a year now and this was the development they had all feared. The Court Of Ghouls had realised that it was only a matter of time before someone got hold of Dr Hendy and forced him to brew them up 'something special'. Galloway knew he had to find Hendy before any new weapons were made from Etherjuice. He turned to the crowd.

"Alright everyone. Settle down now. Tell me, who threw this at the Miccianos?" he asked, holding up the remains of the bottle.

"The Dead Detective, Hank Kane!" shouted a voice deep in the crowd.

"Right, that's good enough for me," said the Sergeant, knowing if he got to Hank, he'd get to Dr Hendy. He didn't even stop to question whoever had shouted out Hank's name. If he had done, he might have uncovered a well-disguised TG.

CHAPTER FIVE

TG IS THE LAW

BACK in his office Hank sat opposite a very frightened Dr Hendy. "You should have told me you sold the Etherjuice secrets to the Miccianos," said Hank. "These guys don't mess about. My guess is that once they had what they needed from you, they froze you out the deal?"

"Something like that. But I only let them know about the weak stuff, none of my special brews."

"These guys are very enterprising, Doc. They'll find a way of replicating all your compounds before long."

"I wish you hadn't used that stuff when you raided *The Cesspit*, Hank. It's only a matter of time before they trace it back to me. And then what will I do?"

"Relax Doc. It may not seem like it now, but you just joined the winning side. Things are going to change around here. Ghostgow's days as a haven for the ghosts of bad guys are nearly over. The city's ill, and corruption is its disease. You and me Doc, we are the cure, in our very different ways. First up, you can't stay here."

"Why not?"

"Because, you're right, it won't take the police or the Miccianos long to trace the Etherjuice grenade back to you. My guess is that the Miccianos are already freed, released by someone close to TG."

"TG? I thought he was on your side!"

"You and me both, Doc."

"So what are you saying, Hank? That we're at war with TG?" asked Dr Hendy, beginning to doubt he was on the right side.

"No, I think we can avoid a war. But for the moment, we can't trust him until we get to the bottom of this."

"What about the police? Couldn't we just level with them?"

Hank explained that the police would never believe that TG was responsible for the chaos the city was sinking into. He was a hero to the police. On the streets, TG *was* the law. They'd do anything on his orders and right now, Hank didn't want to imagine what these orders might be! After all, Hank had discovered through Dr Hendy that TG's dealing in Etherjuice was responsible for attracting all the worst kinds of ghosts to Glasgow. And thanks to the fight with the Miccianos at *The Cesspit*, Hank was sure TG knew that Dr Hendy had told Hank everything.

Just then the phone rang.

"Charlie! Anything happ… calm down…what! No, don't come here. Stay put…"

Tony Falco, who'd been keeping watch on Hank's office from the street, came bursting into the room.

"Hank, we gotta get out of here! They're breaking down the door!"

"Stay put Charlie!" shouted Hank as himself, Dr Hendy and Tony ran up the stairway inside the building until they reached the roof. Hank looked at Tony and Tony looked at Hank. They heard the door downstairs falling in and footsteps clattering up the stairs. Being caught by the police in this city would mean an uncertain fate.

"Stand back!" cried Dr Hendy as he took out two small bottles from a false compartment in the heel of his boot and threw them at the wall. They all ducked down, taking cover against the nearest wall.

BOOOMMM!!!

The wall was simply gone! Hank looked at Dr Hendy in awe.

"Triple Z strength, Hank."

Hank shook his head a little and dust fell off his shoulders. "C'mon," he yelled as the three of them jumped into the back alley behind the building. All around them they could hear screaming! The wild, constant screaming of lots of people; men, woman, old and young. They ran out into the alley and onto Hope Street. Cars, buses, taxis were all crashing into each other and people were running around. A young couple were running past Hank when the girl stopped and stared at him.

"Don't look!" yelled her male companion, "Don't look, keep running!"

Hank stepped forward. "What's going on?" he asked.

The girl looked at him as if frozen to the spot – and then shrieked in absolute terror as she looked at the talking skeleton that was Hank Kane. Her boyfriend picked her up and carried her away, his screams almost matching hers.

"My potion!" shouted Hank to Dr Hendy and he turned to go back to the office. But the police were now in the alleyway, their dogs picking up Hank's scent.

"You don't need it, Hank, look around you!" shouted Hendy.

Everywhere Hank could see humans in sheer terror as they encountered ghosts in varying stages of decay. Suddenly Hank realised what had happened. It was just as Dr Hendy had said when they met in *The Coffee Shop*; too many ghosts had drunk the wrong dosage of Etherjuice. Many of them were now roaming around Hope St and the surrounding area, their flesh dripping from their bones. They had obviously drank enough Etherjuice to look good when they checked in the mirror before they went out. But it had worn off too quickly. So Hank didn't look out of place at all tonight! Fallen flesh mixed with the rain as it ran down the streets.

The police spotted them almost immediately.

"There they are!" shouted one officer.

Hank, Hendy and Tony ran for it.

"Charlie is at Cowcaddens. Run in that direction."

As they ran past a TV shop, Hank could see a news report on the TV screens being read by a newsreader whose face was falling off! That's what Charlie had been trying to tell him on the phone. The ghosts were taking over the human's jobs. But they hadn't worked out how much Etherjuice to take, and it was wearing off too soon. All around him people were screaming that 'The End' had come. Ghosts who'd taken too much Etherjuice were simply exploding all over the city!

Where was TG? thought Hank. Surely he could do *something*. They ran across Renfield Street and suddenly a car appeared out of nowhere and made straight for them. Guns were pointed out of the windows and suddenly they found themselves being shot at. The shots made gigantic holes in the walls they hit. Of course Hank knew he was already dead and that bullets couldn't hurt him so he didn't even try to get out the way. This was the car from the other night and he was determined to see who was in it.

But suddenly Dr Hendy shouted, "Hank, those bullets can do you serious damage! Get out of the way! Quick!"

Hank suddenly felt fear, fear like he hadn't felt since he'd been killed. The car mounted the kerb and machine-guns rattled at them. They ducked just in time, and the car sped off firing at random. Hank watched it drive away and saw ghosts further down the street being hit by machine gun fire and then simply exploding!

"Quick, in here!" shouted Hendy. All three of them ran into the cinema on Renfield Street.

"How can these bullets hurt us, Doc?" asked Hank, as they all slumped down onto the seats inside. "We're all dead anyway!"

"I forgot to mention, Hank," said Hendy, " the real reason the Miccianos wanted the Etherjuice formula was because they wanted to make weapons out of it."

"So, the Miccianos are armed to the teeth with Etherjuice bullets. Great! That's just great. They've worked it out. The city, and its ghosts are at the mercy of a Mafia gang. Great. How many of these Etherjuice hand-grenades do you have?"

"Only what you've got left in your pockets. All this craziness started before I got the chance to make more."

Hank sighed. He reckoned they were safe inside the cinema for the moment. The rain would make it hard for the cops to stay on their scent. Hank went out to the lobby to use the pay phone. He needed to tell Charlie to meet them at the cinema. The line was dead so Hank went back inside. He left the door open, so that some light could come in and so they could hear if anyone else arrived. They all sat down, catching their breaths. Tony spoke first.

"What the devil's going on out there?"

"Don't ask me!" replied Hank. "Ask the city's resident mad scientist over there."

He watched as Dr Hendy pulled a metal wire out of his socks.

"Here, hold this," he said to Hank.

"What is it?"

"For now, it's a radio aerial."

Dr Hendy then pulled a mobile phone from his coat pocket.

"Hank, walk over to the door will you? Try to

get as close to the street as you can without being seen. I'll follow you."

They crouched down and made their way to the entrance. Things seemed to have quietened down. Dr Hendy took a scrap of paper from his wallet and checked it. He dialled some numbers on the phone and then held it to his ear and waited.

"Bingo!" he exclaimed.

"What?" asked Hank.

"Here, listen," said Hendy.

Hank took the phone without having much confidence in it working. He'd never mastered the darned things. But even *he* could manage to put the handset up to his ear. He was surprised to hear Radio Deadbeat blaring out from it! Dr Hendy looked pleased with himself.

"I've transformed that phone into a radio. It's primitive and I'm disappointed that I still need the aerial, very lo-tech, I'm afraid – "

"Stop babbling, Doc I'm trying to hear the news. I wanna know what the heck's going on."

"It's midnight and this is Radio Deadbeat. I'm Jasper Leitch. The headlines today: Edgar Aitken, lead guitar player with *The Phantom's*

Feet, was arrested today for dropping litter in George Square. A spokesman for the band denied it was a publicity stunt designed to enhance the band's 'Bad Boy' image. Sport's news now and in the Ghost Volleyball Championships, the cup final between the Madrid Maniacs and the Paris Pikemen was abandoned tonight when one of the French team crushed the head that was being used as the volleyball with a ferocious smash at the net. Mr Ivan Batty, who was the owner of the head, plans to sue…"

"I don't believe it!" said Hank. "Not a thing about tonight's madness! Hendy, can you get this phone to call this number?"

Hank gave Hendy Charlie's mobile number.

"The networks are down, Hank," said Hendy after trying a few times. He took out a screwdriver from his pocket and fiddled with the inside of the handset and tried again.

"It's ringing now, Hank."

Hank was now really worried about Charlie and Annie. Charlie had told him he'd gone up to Cowcaddens after Annie had called to report some strange happenings. That's all Hank knew.

He waited eagerly for Charlie to answer the phone. It stopped ringing. It had been answered.

"Charlie! You alright?"

"He's alright, Hank. So's Annie. They're with me."

Hank paused. Then he spoke into the phone. "Hello, TG."

CHAPTER SIX

THE MEDICINE MAN

TG told Hank that things were getting back to normal. The ghost police SES squad had made sure that no more Etherjuice was sold from *The Cesspit* and the other few ghost clubs that had sprung up to cater for the influx of ghost tourists. The effects of the Etherjuice that had been sold were now wearing off. The ghosts who'd taken too much and exploded had now been literally swept off the streets! And the ghosts who'd taken too little, had crept back home, embarrassed to have lost their flesh in public, vowing never to mess around with Etherjuice again.

TG agreed to get Charlie and Annie back home right away. Then he'd get round to Hank's office first thing in the morning. He said he had some clearing up to do.

"Are you sure it's safe to go back, Hank?" asked Tony.

"TG said he'd straightened everything out with the cops."

"Can we trust him?" asked Hendy

"No."

"Then why are we heading back?"

"Because I think we're safe while TG needs our help."

"He needs 'help' alright, but from a different sort of doctor than me!" said Dr Hendy.

It was quiet. For the first time in weeks, it was quiet. The madness of a few hours ago had broken like a storm that had been building for a long time. But now, even the rain had calmed down to a light drizzle. They climbed the stairs to Hank's office, dreading the mess the cops might have left. But when they got there, they found the door back on its hinges, and locked.

Hank took out his key, not really expecting it to work – but it did. He opened the door and went in. Spotless! Not a thing out of place, he noted. In fact, if anything, it was tidier than normal! He looked around but couldn't see anything missing. The others walked in behind him. Considering they'd abandoned the office in such a hurry, it looked spotless.

"Everything okay, Mr Kane?"

Hank looked around. It was Kira Walker, the

cleaning lady from Dead Clean, TG's firm that kept the building ship shape.

"Fine, Kira," replied Hank, puzzled.

"Must get going, Mr Kane. Got a lot of work to do tonight. Still, I can't complain, TG is paying us all triple time!"

Triple time? Thought Hank. My, TG must have really wanted the place cleaned up fast.

Tony got a call on his mobile. He listened to a voice that was obviously telling him some good news.

"That's great! Thanks! See you later then."

"What's cheered you up?" asked Hank.

"The ghost police have relaxed the city security for a few hours. Looks like I'm going back to Bandit Heaven, Hank. Well, I'd like to say it's been fun – but I can't! Are we even now Hank? Have I repaid you the favour?"

"So long, Deputy. Just remember I've got friends in Bandit Heaven. Keep your nose clean!"

"So long, Sheriff. Hope this town stays quiet."

And with that, Tony went on his way. Dr Hendy looked at Hank, concerned that he was now Hank's only helper.

"I hope you're not expecting me to replace Tony as your Deputy!"

Hank looked back at Hendy and smiled.

"No, I'd say you'd be more use as a Medicine Man, Doc."

"Why do I not feel comforted by that? Listen, Hank, you might be interested in a wee experiment."

"What do you mean?"

"Where's your radio?"

"Don't blow up my radio, Doc– "

"I know what I'm doing. Now where is it?"

Hank brought the Doctor over to where the radio was. Hendy opened up the back of it with a screwdriver. Hank thought about protesting but decided against it. Dr Hendy had proven nothing but useful so far, so Hank was intrigued.

"There!" said the Doctor. He bent over the radio and fiddled with the tuning. Hank heard all the static between stations until Dr Hendy found what Hank thought was another radio station for ghosts. But when he listened closely he realised that this was actually the ghost police frequency.

"This will allow us to monitor what the ghost

police are up to. You can never be too careful, especially these days," said Dr Hendy.

They played cards for a while, all the time listening to the ghost police on the radio. Things did indeed seem to have quietened down. The ghost police cars were all reporting that the city was almost back to normal. Hank knew that there were forty-eight ghost police cars in 'Ghostgow'. He had some friends on the force, though most of them were suspicious of TG's favourite detective. Hank and the Doctor listened in for some time before they heard anything interesting. But then Hank heard one of the cars calling into the controller.

"Hey Sarge, who is that joker driving out of the police car compound? He nearly smashed right into me!

"Dunno Billy, all our cars are out on patrol."

"But Sarge, I've just passed the compound and this guy came flying out of there! Big American police car,1950s style. Old fashioned music blaring out it."

"Oh, that must be the special cop's car TG brought in from The States."

"Why does he need to bring them in from

anywhere? What's wrong with our cars? Anyway, tell these guys I'll book them for speeding next time they drive like that!"

"Don't be so touchy, Billy, these guys are doing a good job. And, they're pretty tough. Back in 1950s LA, they were the elite squad that put away many of the big gangsters."

"I thought superhero Hank Kane did that single-handedly?"

"Well, I'm sure Hank did his bit, too."

And with that they lost the station as static took over the airwaves. Hank thought about what he'd just heard. If these guys in Ghost Car 49 were who he thought they were, then this case was just beginning. He decided to enjoy the calm before the storm. If Ghostgow thought what had happened tonight was a storm, then the city had seen nothing yet!

Hank felt tired for the first time in days.

"You're sleeping on that couch, Doc. Best get some sleep. I got a feeling we'll need plenty of energy for tomorrow."

CHAPTER SEVEN

FULL KANE STRENGTH

HANK woke up with a start! He checked his bedside clock. It was three o'clock in the morning. He heard the sound of a car engine revving up in the distance. It was the sound of a car racing through its gears. As the noise got closer, he could hear the car's tyres screech as it skidded around corners. He could also make out the sound of jazz music, faint at first, but getting louder as the car got closer.

Hank went over to the window and looked outside. There was no one around. Just then the car skidded onto Gordon Street and Hank saw its windows being wound down. It looked like a 1950s LA police car. He tried to see who was inside. All he knew was that they were armed as he suddenly saw machine guns appearing at each window. As he squinted tightly to catch a glimpse, he realised that the guns were pointed up at his window! Before he had a chance to get out of the way, he was blown back by the force of the bullets that rattled off his bones, breaking many of them.

The firing seemed to go on forever, smashing the office windows and wrecking the walls inside. Everything in the line of fire was smashed to smithereens. Hank lay in the corner, barely conscious. This wasn't normal for ghosts to feel like this. It was as if these bullets were capable of killing dead guys!

Hank's mind was drifting. The room was spinning. Everything was getting darker, and darker until all went black. The sound of Dr Hendy shouting at him seemed miles away in the distance. Hank tried to move but found it impossible. He tried to think straight. Then he just tried to think. He couldn't. He tried to stay awake, fighting the unconsciousness that seemed to smother him until finally he lost the fight. And then the Dead Detective just died. If he'd been alive, he'd have been complaining to TG that this shouldn't be happening.

Dr Hendy crawled over the broken glass to the smashed window. He listened carefully. He could hear the roar of the car getting fainter. He peeked over the window ledge and saw that the street was silent and empty. He ran over to Hank and went to shake him to see if there was any sign of life, so to speak. But Hank's skeleton just crumbled, all the bones disconnecting themselves from each other. Dr Hendy looked round to find TG standing behind him in the room. Dr Hendy wasn't scared. He was angry.

"What are you doing here, TG?" he demanded. "Have you no respect?" TG looked at him, slightly concerned that Hendy appeared not to be afraid of him. But, over the last two or three weeks, TG had been getting used to that. "I'm here to do my job, Doc, I'm here to collect Hank's soul, again."

"You just don't get it, do you?" shouted Hendy, getting to his feet. "There is no soul here! Look around, TG. You see any bewildered soul, floating around, asking you why they've died? No! Nor do I! It was Hank's soul that that hit-squad in the ghost car just murdered!"

Dr Hendy looked at TG with contempt. And he had more to say.

"So, you don't know everything after all, huh? Ask me to explain it to you? Go on. I'm feeling generous. I *might* just share my knowledge with you."

There was silence. Not knowing what was

going on, not being in control of events was something The Grim Reaper had never had to deal with before. But now he was out of his depth for the first time, needing a mad scientist to explain the world to him. TG looked at Hank. This wasn't meant to happen at all. TG knew things had gone haywire earlier. He'd known Charlie and Annie were in great danger.

He knew the chaos the city had suffered that evening was the perfect cover for anyone wanting Hank Kane and his assistants out of the way. TG had raced to Cowcaddens and saved Charlie and Annie from the Miccianos. He'd got there in the nick of time and rescued them. He'd kept his word to Hank and dropped them back home and placed a guard of elite FBI (Friendly But Invisible) agents outside their house.

TG had never heard of dead souls before this current crisis in Ghostgow. But he'd heard enough of it over the last twenty-four hours to last a lifetime. The Court Of Ghouls was looking for him. They wanted an explanation and who could blame them? Their man on the street, TG, was meant to stop this kind of thing from happening. There would have to be an inquiry. There would have to be a fall guy.

Finally TG looked over at Dr Hendy, who'd lifted up a floorboard in the room. The Doctor reached in and picked out what looked like a large toolbox. He brought it over to Hank's remains. TG's mood improved slightly.

"You've got a plan, Doc?"

"No thanks to you, TG."

"How'd you know that toolbox was there?"

"Because I put it there. I've got bits and pieces stashed all over this city, looked after by people I trust. Now watch and learn. Before I start, TG, I want you to carefully place Hank's bones in order, like the right one next to the other and so on, so that he looks like the skeleton we all know and love, instead of a bundle of bones with a funny hat."

"How should I know where all the pieces go?" complained TG.

"Just do it, TG, or you'll have to explain to the Court why their favourite detective is no more."

"I was always terrible at jig-saws," mumbled TG, bending down to start putting Hank back together again.

"So where did Ghost Car 49 get its supply of Grade Triple Z Strength Etherjuice, TG? Did they invent it themselves – or did you sell them the formula?"

"I didn't sell them anything! These guys were cops. Not only were they cops, but they'd heard about Ghostgow's attraction, namely Etherjuice. The Miccianos thought they could muscle in here and make a killing from finding the formula and selling it to anyone with a buck. Plus, they could think of other uses for it, such as weapons and the like. Once they had tricked some ghost tourist into giving them some, they analysed it and made their own crude stuff – "

" – You mean that stuff that was sold through *The Cesspit*?"

"That's right. Once they got their hands on that wonder drug for ghosts, they could call the shots. Ghosts came from all over the place knowing that they didn't need a prescription from me any more. They just needed to make the Miccianos a bit richer. Once these gangsters had that kind of power, it would only be a matter of time before they bribed the police to turn a blind eye to all their criminal activities, just like they did back in LA. And, they discovered that if you experimented with Etherjuice, you could make bullets that could kill ghosts. Frightening huh?"

"None of that would have happened if you hadn't dished out the Etherjuice. Some scientific discoveries are best kept secret."

"I know. I know."

"So where does Ghost Car 49 come into all of this?"

"Like I said, these cops knew the Miccianos and they were a match for them. I figured if I could get them to come here, I'd have...we'd *all* have, some protection. See, back in 1950s LA this elite anti-gangster squad had a running battle with the Miccianos that lasted years - until Hank Kane stormed their mansion single-handedly and killed them all."

"He stole their thunder?"

"And the reward that the mayor had put up for capturing or killing the gang. And just to rub their noses in it, Hank gave the reward to charity."

"Is that why they wanted Hank dead?"

"Maybe."

"So where did they get the Triple Z Strength from?"

"Me. They had to be armed to take on the Miccianos. So I stole some from your lab, or should I say, I got someone else to break in and steal it. I thought arming these guys would turn the war in our favour. I knew things would have to work in our favour. And it did! The Miccianos are all dead. And so are their henchmen. You must have noticed how peaceful the city is?"

"Yeah, but this office wasn't very peaceful last night, was it TG?"

Dr Hendy waited until TG had completed the task of rebuilding Hank's skeleton before opening his toolbox. Wow, thought TG looking at what appeared to be a mini laboratory, complete with smoky potions. There was even a small light on the underside of the lid, which came on when the box was opened.

The Doctor took out three small bottles, similar to the one Hank had thrown when he'd raided *The Cesspit*. The Doctor gently unscrewed what appeared to be a lid and then tilted it upwards. He emptied the powder contained inside onto his hand. He placed the powder carefully on

Hank's skull. He repeated this with the other two Etherjuice hand-grenades. Then he took what looked like a small mobile phone from the box, messed around with the speaker part of it until a small hole appeared. Next, he took out a bottle of smoking liquid and poured it into the phone. The phone started to fizz.

"Here, TG, hold this for a minute."

TG did what he was told, and watched, fascinated. Dr Hendy took another couple of potion bottles out. They contained Etherjuice but the colour was not like any Etherjuice TG had ever seen.

"What's that, Doc? Is that some kind of Grade Triple Z Strength?"

"If I wanted to cremate Hank's remains, then that's just what I'd use! No, dummy, this has no name yet. I've never tested it before. I *hope* it's the antidote to Triple Z Strength. If it works, I'll call it Full Kane Strength."

"And if it doesn't?"

"Then I'll call it TG's Surprise!"

"No, I mean, if it doesn't work, what do we do?"

"We go back to the drawing board. Or should

I say *I* go back to the drawing board. You'll stay far away from my experiments. Look what happened last time you got involved!"

"How long have we got to bring Hank back to 'life'? That is what you're trying to do, isn't it?"

"You've got it all worked out, mate," said Dr Hendy with all the sarcasm he could muster as he poured his new experimental brew all over Hank's remains. He stood up. "Give me the mobile phone, TG." TG did so and the Doctor motioned to him to stand right back.

Hendy took the wire he'd used earlier that evening in the cinema and attached it to the phone, which by now was fizzing wildly. It looked like the phone had a gigantic aerial. He pointed it at Hank's remains, moving forward until the end of the wire touched Hank's rib cage, carefully put back together by TG. Then he dialled a four-digit number on the phone and waited a few seconds. The phone rang once and the room lit up as if some kind of electrical charge had zoomed from the phone, down the aerial and onto Hank's bones.

The bones started smoking and hissing but TG could see that they were fusing together. The

Doctor pressed another four-digit number on the phone and the strength of the charge increased more and more until the phone, the wire and Hank's skeleton all started sparking madly, like a fireworks display! The noise was incredible as sparks flew everywhere until, without any warning, the whole room simply exploded with an enormous bang!

CHAPTER EIGHT

COME IN GHOST CAR 49

THE next morning, Charlie and Annie arrived at Hank's office and knocked on the door. TG let them in.

"What the…?" exclaimed Charlie as he and his sister looked around at what was left of Hank's office.

"What happened, TG?" yelled Annie. She could see that TG was very shaken and his hood was all singed at the front.

Charlie noticed Dr Hendy staggering into the room from the bathroom. He was dusting himself down, shaking bits of glass from his spiky red hair.

"Where's Hank?" Charlie asked.

TG and Dr Hendy exchanged worried glances and Dr Hendy motioned for them to follow him into Hank's bedroom, which they did. There they saw Hank's skeleton lying on the bed. Hank opened his eyes slightly and saw his assistants and their worried expressions. He tried to sit up.

"Here, Hank, drink this," insisted Dr Hendy.

"Thanks, Doc. I've got to get up. Here, help me."

Hendy helped Hank to his feet and Hank put his arm on the Doctor's shoulder and they all walked through to the office area. Hank was determined, no matter how ill he felt, to get to the bottom of recent events. He was sure they were all linked; the hauntings, the influx of visitors, the Etherjuice bootleggers, the chaos of last night and of course, the hit squad in the ghost car.

"Is someone going to tell us what happened here?" asked Annie.

"Let me see," said Hank, coughing slightly as he leaned forward in his chair. "I'd like to piece this case together, bit by bit, just so we don't miss anything. Maybe the emergency is over, maybe it isn't. All I know is these guys who tried to kill me last night – "

"Tried to *kill* you!" said Charlie.

"They did kill him – " corrected the Doctor.

" – They *did* kill him?" said Annie

"Wow, we'll get nowhere fast if we keep this up. Let me summarise where we're at," said Hank.

"Okay. So a few days ago TG tells us what we already knew from the human TV, that there had been an increase in hauntings, right? TG makes us think that it's just a few idiots mucking about and he doesn't want the Court to get too involved. They don't understand TG's business ethics. It all sounds plausible so far. So he asks us all to keep a look out for haunters, all to protect the profits of The Grim Group Ltd.

"But TG, I was on to you from the start. First of all, that ghost car appeared outside my window and it was clearly visible to humans as they were petrified. Now that's news in Ghostgow. But Radio Deadbeat didn't carry the story on the news at all. You run Radio Deadbeat, so I thought you'd kept the story under wraps, to keep the public calm. And the humans who saw the ghost car could always be called drunks, or crazy. It was late at night in the city centre after all. Second, when you briefed us on the case, you never mentioned the ghost car incident."

"I thought you were going to *The Cesspit* that night. I didn't think you'd be in your office. So I didn't think you knew about the ghost car," said TG.

"Exactly. The next day, I get a nice surprise. I

hear my old 'friend', Tony Falco is back in town. And guess what? He tries to sell me some Etherjuice. I 'questioned' him as to how he came to have it. And he told me he broke into Hendy's lab and stole it. He swore it was a legal break-in because he'd been assured by TG that it was all for the public good."

"TG! How could you?" yelled Annie.

"So now I've worked out that TG's story about being concerned with all the hauntings is a smokescreen. He's really trying to cover up the fact that the city is out of control, the streets flooded with Etherjuice. The hauntings weren't done by ghosts having a laugh. They were done by ghosts who'd taken the wrong dosage of Etherjuice and so become visible now and again to humans."

"So," said Charlie, TG realised that the increase in the reported number of hauntings was actually a warning that more and more ghosts were on the juice?"

"That's right, Charlie. TG, you wanna fill us in from here?"

TG told them everything that he'd confessed to Dr Hendy the night before.

"But none of that explains why Ghost Car 49 wants Hank dead," insisted Charlie. "I don't think they'd want to kill you just 'cause you beat them to an arrest or the killing of the Miccianos. You were all cops right? They might sulk that you got the glory, but it doesn't add up that they'd want you dead for that!"

Hank thought about that. He agreed with Charlie. There must be something that TG was not telling them.

"Let's put it out on the radio, Dr Hendy," said Hank.

Annie looked puzzled. The Doctor put on the radio and tuned it to the ghost police frequency. Charlie and Annie looked at the Doctor in awe. Wow, what a cool guy, they thought. They all strained to hear what was being said. TG however, just looked more and more uncomfortable. Hank kept watching him and that didn't help. They heard lots of police chatter, boring stuff. They mulled over the case with one ear fixed on the radio. About an hour later an interesting conversation started.

"Come in Ghost Car 49. Come in...do you read me? This is control. Come in." This controller was not the Glasgow sergeant Hank and Hendy had heard the previous evening. This guy had an American accent. Hank recognised it. He listened even more intently now.

"Ghost Car 49 here, Captain Curtis."

"Hey Burt what's going on. Did you get Kane?"

"Right between the eyes, Captain. He's history."

"Good work fellas. Now all we gotta do is find that lousy Doctor. He's the last man with Etherjuice in his possession."

"Apart from us, Captain!"

And the airwaves were filled with static and laughter.

"Burt, go back to Kane's place. The Doctor must be there somewhere. We've searched the whole city. I've told the Ghostgow cops that the Doctor is a mad scientist, and he's out to blow the whole place up. They saw what he did to Kane's Ghost the other night."

"What about TG? He's their hero ain't he?"

"Not since we told them about TG bringing in the Miccianos to Ghostgow! Man, are they mad!"

CHAPTER NINE

GHOST KILLERS

TG had turned off the radio. "I've got a plan," he announced.

"Sit down TG, we've had enough of your plans," said Dr Hendy.

"Why you – listen to me wise guy – "

Hank stood up. "Like he said, TG, sit down. You don't have the muscle anymore. The Court has a warrant out for your arrest. The cops have seen through you. Ghost Car 49 is armed to the teeth. You're a liability. In fact, Dr Hendy, I think we should put TG under arrest. Read him his rights, Deputy!"

"Okay, here's your rights. You have none."

TG went to move but the Doctor pointed his mobile phone at him.

"Freeze!"

TG guessed that Hendy's phone was loaded with lethal Etherjuice. He did as he was told.

"Put the scythe down. Kick it in front of you and step back, TG." The Doctor was enjoying this. It was revenge for having had to watch TG take all the glory for the discovery of

Etherjuice. Why shouldn't he enjoy this moment?

"Charlie? Annie? Inside that drawer are bottles of EJ. Take them out and aim them at TG. If he moves, let him have it, okay?"

"Okay," said Charlie. He imagined doing a school report after the holidays and describing this scene, the one where he had The Grim Reaper under arrest. Somehow, all he saw was that he'd get into a lot of trouble for writing about something so bizarre!

"What now, Hank?" asked TG. "You'll need a hell of a plan to get out of this one and something tells me you don't have one."

"Maybe, maybe not. But whatever, happens, you're going down with us, TG. All I know right now, is that we are going to wait for Ghost Car 49 to come back here. They are going to come in, looking for Triple Z Strength and any other Etherjuice they can find. They want it? We'll give 'em it! Charlie and Annie, you'll be posted on the corner of Union Street and Gordon Street, keeping a look out. The minute you see the car, call me. Then you go straight to the Court Of Ghouls with the whole story, okay? Doctor, think of a way of tying up TG.

"Oh, I've thought of a million ways," said Hendy. He pulled out his now famous wire, keeping his phone pointed at TG the whole time.

"Turn around, TG," he said and TG, still coming to terms with his spectacular fall from a high, did so, without complaint. Dr Hendy tied TG's hands together and forced TG to squat on the floor. Then he tied his feet together with some more wire.

"Go on, TG, try and move!" shouted Dr Hendy. When TG did so, the wire flashed with an electrical charge, causing TG pain. The wire was coated with very special Etherjuice. The Doctor's mobile lab, the toolbox, had come in very handy indeed.

Dr Hendy had been working furiously with his toolbox for the last few hours. He knew Ghost Car 49 would be here any minute. Luckily, he carried all the formulas in his memory so it had been quite easy to make some serious weapons from the formulas in his head and the bits and pieces in his toolbox. Hank began to put some bottles in his pockets. Soon they were packed with Ghost Killing Juice Grenades, as Dr Hendy called them.

Hank looked around the room. "Doc, can we place some of these things in dangerous areas around the place?"

TG looked appalled! "Hank!" he protested, "You can't blow this place up! Do you have any idea the trouble I went to in order to recreate your 1950s office?"

Hank ignored him and the Doctor set about booby-trapping the place. Hank noticed that he had a massive container with a liquid smoking away inside it.

"Looks nasty, Doc. What is it?"

"Oh, just some special petrol for Ghost Car 49. Wouldn't want it to run out now, would we?"

"Good. Now, call Charlie and tell him you're going to hide this next to the litterbin outside the newsagents. When the ghost car comes, all four of these guys will want to grab some kind of trophy from my office."

"Bones," whispered TG

"What?"

"Bones, that's the ultimate trophy for ghost killers. They like to show off the bones of ghosts they kill. If you scatter some near the window, you'll get all four of them in here."

"I can think of a few bones I'd like to scatter!" said the Dr, looking at TG.

"I can get you some," whispered TG.

"What?"

"I said I can get you some bones. Untie me and I'll get you some bones. I am The Grim Reaper after all."

"No way, TG. Tell Charlie where they are and he'll bring them," said Hank

Hank put the phone to TG's ear and TG told Charlie. Charlie was up the stairs within five minutes, with the bag of bones. He passed them to Hank and raced back downstairs to get to his lookout post. Hank spread the bones out all over the floor, making it look like he'd been blown to pieces.

"Hank, your hat!" called the Doctor as he came back up the stairs after leaving the 'petrol' down at the litter-bin for Charlie.

"Oh yeah," said Hank as he put the finishing touch to the bones by placing his hat on the skull.

The Doctor was now climbing into the gap between the ceiling and the roof.

"What are you doing now, Doc?"

"Just 'fixing' the sprinklers, Hank. You never know but with all this Etherjuice, there might be a fire!"

"Good thinking. 'Fix' the ones on the staircase too!" he shouted up to the Doctor.

"Done!" shouted back Hendy.

Dr Hendy came into the room where Hank was looking out the window.

"What about him?" he said, nodding his head towards TG.

"Can you make a weak version of Juice? Just strong enough to knock him out till we get him to the Court?"

Dr Hendy walked over to TG, taking a couple of pills from his wallet. TG turned his head away in resistance.

"Now, now, TG, take these. They don't hurt a bit. You do want to get better, don't you? Morally I mean!" He forced the tablets into TG's mouth and he fell asleep immediately.

Hank's phone went. It was Charlie.

"Quick Doc!" shouted Hank throwing the

receiver down. "It's time to get outta here! Here, help me with TG!"

"Wait, let me set up the aerials." Hendy pulled a bundle of wires from under Hank's floorboards. He quickly set them up all around the room, coating some with explosive Triple Z and some with Transmitter Etherjuice.

The Doctor and Hank carried TG out the back way, out the Ghost Exit, and found themselves in the alleyway. They heard the screech of Ghost Car 49 as it sped into Gordon Street. No gunfire this time, just laughter as the ghost car cops joked, on their way up the stairs to Hank's office.

Hank and the Doctor hid TG in the alley and ran around to Central Station where they climbed up onto the roof so that they could get a view of Hank's office. Hank could see right into the office and he saw all four of the guys holding up the bones that were scattered there. Why, one of them was even trying on his hat! He looked at Dr Hendy, who had five mobile phones all lined up on a ledge, pointing at the office.

Hank looked down at the street. It was empty.

He'd told Charlie to alert the human police that there was an unsafe building and cordon off the whole area. Even the trains had stopped. He turned to Hendy.

Just then he saw Charlie run over to the litterbin. He grabbed the container left for him by the Doctor and proceeded to empty it into the petrol tank of Ghost Car 49. Hank watched until Charlie was well away from Gordon Street.

"You ready, Doc? We ain't got all day."

"Ready when you are Hank."

Hank peered through a pair of binoculars he'd grabbed on his way out of his office. He saw all four of the cops sitting down. One of them was looking at one of the wire aerials. He seemed amused by it. He got up and went over to it. Hank shouted to Hendy.

"Now!"

Hendy pressed the send button on all the phones.

BOOOOMMMMMM!!!!!!

The whole building went up in smoke – and then came down in pieces. Hank saw two of the guys running down what was left of the staircase.

"The sprinklers, Doc!"

Hendy hit another phone and the sprinklers came on. But it wasn't water it poured onto the fleeing bad guys – it was Triple Z. Hank could see through the binoculars that the Triple Z simply melted the flesh and disintegrated the bones of the ghost car cops.

Just then, a ghost in an LA police uniform ran into Gordon Street. He stood staring at the mess. A crowd of Ghostgow cops came round the corner.

"There he is!" they shouted.

The LA cop ran to Ghost Car 49, followed by the Glasgow human cops. The LA cop got in. Hank guessed him to be the controller they had heard on the police radio last night. Oh no, thought Hank, the local cops will be blown up as well when the engine of the car is started, thanks to Dr Hendy's 'petrol'! Suddenly, Charlie came on the scene.

"Charlie!" shouted Hank

"Get back!" shouted Charlie to the local cops. Hank couldn't hear what Charlie was saying but it was making sense to the local cops. They all started running in the opposite direction. Only the LA cop was left in the car. He started the engine. Charlie and the local cops had just reached the corner, when

 BOOOOMMMMM!!!!!

Ghost Car 49 had screeched round its last corner.

CHAPTER TEN

A NEW ASSISTANT

THE Court Of Ghouls had witnessed everything. They'd been with the guys that were running after the LA cop that got into the car. Turned out that the ghost car cops had wanted Hank dead because they had never really been the enemies of the Micciano crime family. They'd been partners. That was why, back in 1950s LA, this elite team of cops never seemed to catch the Miccianos, 'cause they didn't want them caught! Hank had been investigating them not long before he died and they knew he was on to them.

TG knew none of this. He simply thought the ghost car cops were the toughest there was. So he let them into Ghostgow. He had no idea they would team up with the Miccianos. He thought they would protect the city from them. That's why things went crazy. The cops and robbers had been on the same side all along. And the corrupt cops in Ghost Car 49 knew it was just a matter of time before Hank rumbled the whole scam. That's why he 'had to go'.

"So, Dr Hendy," said the vampire judge, "you claim that every ounce of Etherjuice is accounted for in our vaults?"

"Yes, sir!"

"Well, you really have redeemed yourself. But we need you to stick around a while longer. We wouldn't know where to start should a similar crisis grip this city again."

"I understand, sir."

"However, you will now be officially recognised as the true inventor of Etherjuice."

"Thank you, sir."

"Well Mr Kane. Let's keep this short. You saved the city, yada, yada, yada. And we are very grateful. But the way you raided *The Cesspit* – with no warrant - that was too dangerous for the guys in Detective Heaven. However, your stay here might be a little more enjoyable now that you have another new assistant, someone who really needs training. Not in detective work, but in decency, morality and lots of other things that make ghosts…more pleasant. Bring in Mr Kane's new assistant."

And in came TG, in Etherjuice handcuffs.

CHAPTER ELEVEN

EVEN THE MIGHTY FALL

AS they walked down the steps of the Court, Hank pulling the cuffed TG along, as if he was under arrest. Charlie and Annie couldn't help laughing.

"Looks like the tables have been turned, TG!" they said

"Let this be a lesson to you, kids. Even the mighty fall," said TG, "but I'll be back!"

"TG?" said Hank.

"Yes?" said TG, sounding bored.

"The Court did say that you had to take my advice, no questions answered, did they not?"

"I can see where this is going! Yes, they did say that."

"Well, do you know what I think you need? I think you need some lessons in discipline," he said winking at Charlie and Annie, adding, "any suggestions, guys?"

"Ballet dancing," giggled Annie, "I hear it's also great for posture!"

"Elocution lessons!" said Charlie, "You *do* talk funny, TG!"

"Yoga!" suggested Annie.

And so the list went on, all the way back to Hank's office in Gordon Street.

"Ballet, you say, very interesting, Annie…" said Hank.

OTHER TITLES IN THE DEAD DETECTIVE SERIES:

DEAD AND UNBURIED

Los Angeles 1953... and Private Detective Hank Kane doesn't know what's hit him. Lying face down on the same street he was just running down, he realises he's been shot. But instead of the morgue, Hank finds himself in the Court of Ghouls, in front of a Vampire judge and a jury of ghosts! He's on trial for cheating on his last case. His punishment? To get back to 'life' and solve a case honestly. Lippy 12-year-old Charlie Christian is assigned as his apprentice detective! The question is not, "will they solve the case?" but "will they solve it honestly?"

SIX FEET UNDER

Hank falls and knocks himself out while chasing a thief from his office. He's forgotten to take his "medicine bottle" with him and his flesh starts disappearing, revealing his bony white skeleton underneath. Everybody is talking about the "well-dressed Skeleton" found lying in the street. His old-fashioned 1940s clothes and hat look very strange. The police, after forensic tests, have the body buried. Is this really the end of Hank Cane? It will be, unless Charlie can work out Hank's secret code in the letter in his desk drawer, marked "ONLY TO BE OPENED IN AN EMERGENCY".

If this isn't an emergency what is? But can Charlie handle all the secrets in the letter?

DEAD LOSS

Hank gets a visit from the ghost of murder victim Tony Falco, begging for help. Tony, a cat burglar, had stolen jewels on him when he died and the Court of Ghouls won't let Tony into Bandit Heaven until he returns them. Just one problem though – no-one found Falco's body. It's lost! Hank thinks that the Grim Reaper might have some clues. His apprentice, Charlie, is desperate to solve the case without help of any "dead guys", but he disappears! Now the Grim Reaper and Falco have a body full of loot to find – and the apprentice too!

THROW AWAY THE KEY

"Help me... please, help me!" A voice identifying itself only as "The Prisoner" keeps calling Hank's phone, pleading for help. Despite being asked why, the panicking voice just keeps calling. Charlie introduces Hank to the latest technology in phone tapping and they listen carefully to the background noises, searching for clues. They get worried when they begin to recognise some sounds, which are too familar for comfort. The Prisoner is very, very close to home!!

A Corpse seen in 1940's Los Angeles turns up in 2002, singing on TV! The strangest coincidence – or is Hank's old flame haunting him. She was a great detective who ended up in Sleuth Heaven – so, why give that up just to sing? Charlie sees the romantic side of Hank and wants to throw up! How can they solve cases with Hank staring at the TV all night? For the first time, Charlie has to take the calls at Hank's office. At last, the Kid can prove his worth, and he resolves to break the case of *The Corpse That Sang*.

THE DEAD DETECTIVE SERIES

www.booksnoir.com

Hey guys! Hank Kane here. Check out my website www.deaddetective.com *to keep up to date with my interactive e-book* Web of Intrigue, *an internet adventure where you, the reader, can help me on the case.*

P.S. You'd better be good!